Oliver

Written by Hilary McKay

Illustrated by Rupert Van Wyk

Collins

Chapter 1

Nearly 200 years ago, a baby was born –
a baby boy.

His mother died so quickly that she didn't have
time to give him a name.

But he was given a name anyway.

His name was Oliver Twist.

This is the story of Oliver Twist.

Oliver was born in a workhouse.

In those days, when the poorest of poor people
had nothing left to keep them alive – no home,
no money, no family, no hope – they were sent to
the workhouse. People of all ages were sent there,
the very young and the very old – sent there to
work hard making things like sacks or clothes.
Workhouses were a little better than prisons,
but not very much. There were a few good ones,
where people were given warm food and a bed.
But there were many, many bad ones.

Oliver's workhouse was run by a man called Mr Bumble and it was one of the worst. People starved to death in that place and Mr Bumble was pleased when they did. He pretended he wasn't, but he was.

Dead people didn't need dinners.

If you could call it dinner.

In Mr Bumble's workhouse, the meals never changed. Gruel was served three times a day. Gruel was a sort of watery porridge – it didn't fill you up and it didn't make you grow. You could just about stay alive on gruel, if you were lucky.

Oliver must have been lucky because he just about stayed alive.

When Oliver was nine years old, he was about the size of a boy of six and he was as hungry as a starving tiger.

So were all the other boys in the workhouse. They were hungrier than they could bear and, one day, they made up their minds to ask for more gruel. Somehow Oliver got the job of asking.

5

So he did, and it took some courage.

Oliver walked up to the fat man who gave out the gruel and he said, "Please sir, I want some more."

If Oliver had said, "Please sir, I want Mr Bumble stuffed and roasted with plenty of gravy," there could not have been more fuss. Mr Bumble and all his helpers went wild with rage. They pushed poor Oliver into the cellar while they thought about what to do with him.

They thought of selling him to the chimney sweeper who had accidentally killed three boys already by making them climb up chimneys with fires underneath.

They thought of sending him to sea and hoping he would drown.

And then they thought of selling him to Mr Sowerberry, and that's what they did.

Chapter 2

Mr Sowerberry was an undertaker.
When somebody died, he was the person who
was sent for. He was a very useful man.

He measured the dead person with his tape
measure to see how big to make their coffin.

He hammered together the wooden coffin pieces
in his coffin shop.

Then he put the body in the coffin and took it to
the graveyard where he had sorted out a hole.

Oliver's new job was to help Mr Sowerberry and he didn't like it. Not the sadness, nor the dead people, nor his little bed on the coffin shop floor amongst the half-made coffins.

Oliver also didn't like Noah, the big boy who helped Mr Sowerberry. Noah said awful things about Oliver's poor dead mother.

Oliver tried to stop him, but he couldn't. Noah was stronger and Oliver always lost their battles. So in the end, he ran away.

Chapter 3

He ran all the way to London. It took him a week.
When he got there, he sat down on a doorstep
and was miserable. His feet were sore. He was very
tired and very hungry and very, very lonely.

Oliver sat on the doorstep for a long time before
he noticed that someone was looking at him.
It was a boy, not much older than Oliver. A rough,
tough, bouncy-looking boy whose friends called
him the Artful Dodger.

The Artful Dodger didn't just look at Oliver. He came across and spoke to him. And five minutes later he was buying Oliver his breakfast. Ham sandwiches, the best breakfast that Oliver had ever eaten.

That was how Oliver and the Artful Dodger became friends, and they talked, as friends do. Oliver told him all about the workhouse and Mr Bumble and the coffin shop. The Artful Dodger explained that his real name was Jack and that he lived with an old man called Fagin, and several other boys. And he said that Oliver could come home with him if he liked, so Oliver did.

It was an old, half-broken house in such
a dark muddle of dirty streets that Oliver nearly
ran away. But he didn't. He went inside instead.

And there was Fagin.

Old, old, old!

Strange, strange, strange!

Cooking sausages over the smoky fire.

12

Oliver was used to odd places, but this room was
the oddest he had ever seen. There were several
ragged boys. There was a big girl called Nancy
in a red dress who was singing and cutting
up bread. And hung like flags all across the room
were bright-coloured handkerchiefs. Oliver could
see that they were fine silk handkerchiefs, the sort
that only very rich people could buy. That was
strange because Fagin didn't look rich. Neither did
any of the other people in the room.

Oliver didn't know what to think. He sat in a corner, too tired to even try.

After a while, Nancy brought him some sausages.

"Thank you," said Oliver politely.

Not many people were polite to Nancy. She smiled at Oliver and ruffled his hair. Oliver smiled back, ate his sausages and fell asleep.

Chapter 4

When he woke in the morning, the room was
empty, except for old Fagin who was sorting
through a box of things that shone. Watches and
rings and bracelets and things. Oliver thought
they were beautiful. He didn't guess where they
came from. Even when the boys came home and
showed Oliver the game they played with Fagin,
he didn't guess.

The game was this:

Fagin filled his pockets with treasures – watches, money, bright pocket handkerchiefs. Then up and down the room he stepped, and after him came the boys, dodging, ducking, dancing, trying not to explode with laughter as very, very cleverly they picked the treasures from Fagin's pockets, without him catching them.

It was a better game than hide-and-seek, better than a treasure hunt, better than tag.

It was a game to teach boys how to steal, but
Oliver didn't know that. He thought it was good
fun, and he soon joined in. He got quite good at it!

That pleased Fagin and Fagin's gang.
Because that's what it was: a gang. The boys,
the merry Artful Dodger, Nancy who was so kind.
Even Bull's-eye, the bad-tempered dog.

All Fagin's gang. Thieves. Pickpockets. That was
what they were.

Some of them were proud of it. Some, like Nancy, hated it. The Artful Dodger said it was fair; if he didn't steal things then someone else would.
But all of them did it. Fagin made them.
Fagin had terrible ways of punishing people who didn't do what he said.

Oliver didn't guess any of this until the first day the gang took him on to the streets.

Then, outside a bookshop, everything became clear.

An old gentleman was standing at the window, looking at the books. The Artful Dodger, who was just beside him, grinned at Oliver.

Then, right before Oliver's astonished eyes, into the old gentleman's pocket went the Artful Dodger's hand! Out it came with a beautiful red silk handkerchief.

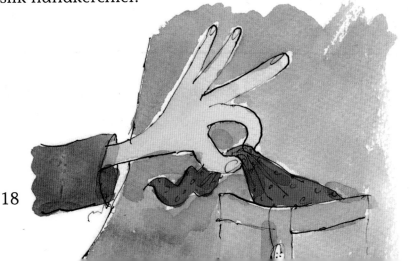

Then Oliver didn't just guess. He knew.

And he stood and stared.

"HEY!" cried the old gentleman.

Where was the Artful Dodger? Gone! The other boys? Vanished!

Oliver turned and ran.

"Stop, thief!" called the old gentleman and he began to run after him. So did many other people, all calling, "STOP, THIEF!"

Bang! Oliver tumbled face down in the muddy
street. He didn't stay there long. A dozen hands
grabbed him and dragged him to his feet again.
A dozen voices shouted, "Here's the thief!"

Oliver tried to speak but he couldn't. His head
was hurting and there was blood in his eyes.
His stomach felt sick and his legs were wobbly.
He was so dizzy he swayed, but just before
he fainted he heard the old gentleman's voice,
"Poor fellow. Don't hurt him!"

Then he didn't hear anything more.

Chapter 5

When Oliver woke up, the world had changed.
He was in a clean bed, in a warm quiet house.

The old gentleman's house.

And there was the old gentleman, Mr Brownlow,
and a smiling lady bringing supper on a tray.

Days turned into weeks. Oliver was happier than he'd ever been. He felt well, he was busy and surrounded by kind people – the kindest of all was Mr Brownlow. He and Oliver became friends. Oliver learnt to read and write, to dig in the garden, to make jokes and plans. The more he learnt, the happier he was and the more the people of the house liked him.

In fact, they said they couldn't manage without him.

It was as if Oliver had lived there always. A home at last.

There seemed nothing to stop him living happily ever after.

But there was.

Old Fagin was very afraid, and so were the boys. Punishments were very hard for gangs of thieves like them.

"What if Oliver tells?" they asked. "Tells where we are! Tells what we do! What will happen then?"

"Oliver would never tell," said Nancy, but the others didn't agree. Especially Fagin.

"He won't tell if I've got him here," said Fagin. So he tracked down Oliver and he made a plan.

Oliver must be kidnapped and Nancy must do it.

"I won't," said Nancy.

"You will," said Fagin. He had terrible red eyes and hands like claws. He stood very close to Nancy and he said, "You'll do it."

And Nancy was frightened.

"Or else!" whispered Fagin.

So Nancy put a dark shawl over her red dress, she hid her eyes that were red from crying and she waited in the street near where Oliver lived. When he came out on to the street, she swooped him up in her arms.

"My little brother!" she cried, and swept him away under the big dark shawl.

It was the worst of all nightmares.

Oliver was back with old Fagin.

The boys said, "Phew!"

The Artful Dodger explained to Oliver how sensible it was to steal things before someone else got them instead.

Fagin grinned and told his dog Bull's-eye what to do if Oliver tried to get away.

Bull's-eye showed Oliver his teeth and his fur stood up in a line along his back.

Everyone agreed that Nancy had done a very good job indeed.

Except Nancy.

"I thought you were my friend," said Oliver to Nancy.

Chapter 6

Days and days and days went past. Nancy never sang any more. Oliver grew thin and pale. Nancy looked at him and she couldn't bear it.

That was why she went and found kind Mr Brownlow.

So it was Nancy who told, not Oliver. She told about Fagin and his gang. Where they were, and what they did, and how they were keeping Oliver a prisoner.

And so Oliver was rescued.

But Nancy vanished. No one except Fagin ever knew what happened to her.

Fagin was hunted and caught and punished at last.

Bull's-eye ran away.

But the boys weren't caught. They hid themselves amongst the tangled streets of London until all the trouble was over. And then they came out.

The Artful Dodger went off to Australia. He liked
it there with the kangaroos and goldmines.
His grin became merrier than ever and he forgot
about pocket handkerchiefs. They weren't
the fashion in Australia anyway.

The other boys scattered, some good, some bad.

Oliver never saw any of them again, but he never
forgot them.

The ragged boys in the muddy streets.

The Artful Dodger's wink.

Old Fagin cooking sausages in the shadowy room.

The bright flags of silk handkerchiefs.

Bull's-eye the dog.

Smiling Nancy.

Nancy singing.

He didn't forget the bed in the coffin shop and
Mr Sowerberry, kneeling with his tape measure.

Nor Mr Bumble and the gruel pot, and
the hungry faces watching.

Please sir, I want some more.

Sometimes they seemed to Oliver like people in a story.

The Story of Oliver Twist.

One day, thought Oliver, I'll write it down.

And he did!

WANTED

His name is
OLIVER TWIST.
If found, grab him
and bring him back to
Old Fagin and his gang.

DO NOT SPEAK TO HIM.

Reward: a silk handkerchief

LOST BOY

Have you seen this boy?

His name is **Oliver Twist**.

He is aged 9, but is very small
for his age.

He is a kind and gentle fellow – we are
finding it hard to manage without him.

He was last seen walking along Victoria
Street where he lives.

**If found, please contact
Mr Brownlow at 20 Victoria Street.**

Ideas for reading

Written by Clare Dowdall, PhD
Lecturer and Primary Literacy Consultant

Reading objectives:
- discuss and clarify the meanings of words, linking new meanings to known vocabulary
- explain and discuss their understanding of books, both those that they listen to and those that they read for themselves
- make inferences on the basis of what is being said and done

Spoken language objectives:
- give well-structured descriptions, explanations and narratives for different purposes, including for expressing feelings
- participate in discussions, presentations, performances, role play, improvisations and debates
- use spoken language to develop understanding through speculating, hypothesising, imagining and exploring ideas

Curriculum links: History; Citizenship

Resources: whiteboard, internet, DVDs about Victorian London

Interest words: pickpockets, gruel, courage, undertaker, artful, punishments, handkerchiefs

Word count: 2,088

Build a context for reading
- Ask children if they know the famous story *Oliver Twist* by Charles Dickens, or if they've seen a film or musical version of it. Explain that the original book was written over 150 years ago in Victorian Times and that this is a shortened version written for children nowadays.
- Ask children to predict what it was like in Victorian times and make notes on a whiteboard.
- Show the children the illustration of Oliver Twist on the front cover. Ask what they can work out from the picture, e.g. *he wants food.*
- Read the blurb with the children. Ask children to suggest what a "band of young pickpockets" is and establish that they are child-thieves who steal from pockets.

Understand and apply reading strategies
- Walk through the book together. Ask children to notice how it is organised in chapters and to look at the illustrations to get a flavour of what will happen in this story.
- Ask children to read pp2–3 quietly, looking for three facts about Oliver. Help children to recount their ideas.